Lil Mouse Is in the House!

Dan Gutman

Pictures by
Jim Paillot

HARPER
An Imprint of HarperCollinsPublishers

To Emma

My Weirder-est School #12: Lil Mouse Is in the House!

Text copyright © 2022 by Dan Gutman

Illustrations copyright © 2022 Jim Paillot

All rights reserved. Printed in the United States of America.

Library of Congress Control Number: 2022940763
ISBN 978-0-06-291088-2 (pbk bdg) — ISBN 978-0-06-291089-9 (trade bdg)

Typography by Laura Mock
22 23 24 25 26 PC/LSCH 10 9 8 7 6 5 4 3 2 1
❖
First Edition

Contents

Map

1001 Insults
For All Occasions

math

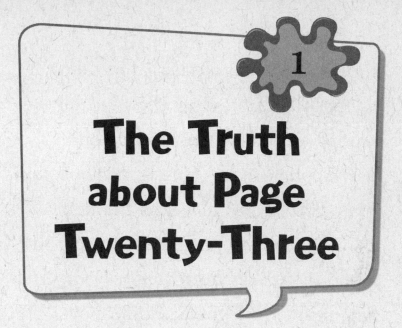

The Truth about Page Twenty-Three

My name is A.J. and I know what you're thinking. You're thinking about clams. Because that's what I'm thinking about.

The other day my mom said I looked like I was happy as a clam. What?! How does *she* know that clams are happy? I bet there are a lot of sad clams out there. I know that if I was a clam, I'd be sad. Who wants to sit around in the mud all day waiting for some walrus to eat you?

The point is, it was June 1, and you know what *that* means. It means the next day would be June 2! June 1 also means that school is almost over for the year. And *that* means third grade is almost over.

YAY!*

Boy, third grade sure took a *long* time! I feel like I've been in third grade for fourteen years.

I had just put my backpack in my cubby when our teacher, Mr. Cooper, came flying into the room. And I *do* mean flying.

*That's also "YAY" spelled backward.

Mr. Cooper thinks he's a superhero, and he wears a cape. That's weird. As usual, he tripped over somebody's umbrella, fell down, and almost took out a row of desks.

"I'm fine!" Mr. Cooper said as he brushed the dirt off his pants.

Then, like every day, we pledged the allegiance and did Word of the Day.

"Okay," said Mr. Cooper, "turn to page twenty-three in your math books."

Ugh. I hate math. Why do we need math when we have calculators?

I didn't bother getting out my math book or turning to page twenty-three. Why should I? Every time Mr. Cooper tells us to turn to page twenty-three in our math books, there's some interruption. It's always an announcement over the loudspeaker telling us to go to the all-porpoise room or the playground for a surprise assembly.

Mr. Cooper has been trying to teach us page twenty-three all year. I'm sure it's some really hard math problem. So I just sat there while everybody else got out their math books.

"A.J.," said Mr. Cooper, "why aren't you taking out your math book?"

"What's the point?" I replied. "There's gonna be an announcement. You'll see."

I looked at the loudspeaker on the wall. There was no announcement.

Andrea Young, this annoying girl with

curly brown hair, got out her math book and turned to page twenty-three.

Ryan, who will eat anything, got out his math book and turned to page twenty-three.

Michael, who never ties his shoes, got out his math book and turned to page twenty-three.

I waited.

And waited. And waited.

No announcement! I was starting to get nervous.

Neil, who we call the nude kid even though he wears clothes, got out his math book and turned to page twenty-three.

Crybaby Emily got out her math book

and turned to page twenty-three.

Alexia, this girl who rides a skateboard all the time, got out her math book and turned to page twenty-three.

Everybody was taking out their math books and turning to page twenty-three. Everybody except me.

"A.J.," said Mr. Cooper, "there isn't going to be an announcement this morning. I checked with the office. Please take out your math book and turn to page twenty-three."

"No!" I said.

Mr. Cooper put his hands on his hips. When a grown-up puts their hands on their hips, you know they're mad at you.

Nobody knows why.

"Dude," Ryan whispered to me, "you won't *believe* what's on page twenty-three."

"It's gonna blow your mind, A.J.," said Michael.

Ryan and Michael usually know what they're talking about. So I took out my math book. I turned to page twenty-three.

And you'll never believe in a million hundred years what was on page twenty-three.

I'm not gonna tell you.

Okay, okay. I'll tell you. It said . . .

2 + 2 = ?

WHAT?! Are you kidding me? *That's* what's on page twenty-three? All these years I've been worried about what was on page twenty-three, and it was just $2 + 2 = ?$ Any dumbhead knows what $2 + 2$ is.

"FOUR!" everybody shouted.

Mr. Cooper closed his math book.

"Very good," he said. "Now that we've finished page twenty-three, I think you kids are ready for fourth grade."

You'll never believe what happened next.

An announcement came over the loud-speaker!

But I'm not going to tell you what it was.

Okay, okay, I'll tell you. But you have to read the next chapter. So nah-nah-nah boo-boo on you.

All the Good Ones Are Dead

The announcement was from Mrs. Patty, our school secretary.

"Third graders," said Mrs. Patty, "please report to the media center."

We walked a million hundred miles to the media center, which used to be called *the library*, but they changed the name. Nobody knows why.

Mrs. Roopy was waiting for us at the door. She's our media specialist. She used to be called *the librarian*, but they changed the name. Nobody knows why.

"Good morning, everyone," said Mrs. Roopy. "I'm so excited that you kids are graduating from third grade! Congratulations! I have some good news and some

better news for you."

"What's the good news?" asked Neil.

"The good news is that I'm going to be in charge of your graduation!"

"YAY!" we all shouted.

"What's the better news?" asked Alexia.

"The better news is that Mrs. Stoker said I could bring in a guest speaker for your graduation."

"YAY!" we all shouted.

Mrs. Stoker is our new principal. The principal used to be Mr. Klutz, but he retired.

A couple of years ago, I went to my sister's graduation, so I know that graduations are a total snoozefest. You have to sit around for a million hundred hours waiting for your name to be called. Then they hand you this piece of paper that your parents stick in your memory box for the rest of your life. Snore.

"Hang on," said Mrs. Roopy. "I'll be right back. I have to make a quick phone call."

She dashed out of the room. So I did what I always do when there are no teachers around. I stood up on my chair and shook my butt at the class.

"Arlo, sit down," said Andrea, rolling her eyes. She calls me by my real name because she knows I don't like it.

A few minutes later, Mrs. Roopy came back. The weird thing was she didn't look like Mrs. Roopy anymore. She was dressed like a man with a bushy mustache, glasses, and a jacket and tie. She must have stuffed a pillow under her shirt because she looked a lot bigger.

"Why are you dressed like that, Mrs. Roopy?" asked Ryan.

"Who's Mrs. Roopy?" said Mrs. Roopy. "Never heard of her. My name is Teddy  Roosevelt. I was the twenty-sixth president of the United States. My face is on Mount Rushmore."

Mrs. Roopy is loopy. Teddy Roosevelt died like a million hundred years ago. We all knew it was just Mrs. Roopy dressed up like Teddy Roosevelt.

Well, *almost* all of us knew it.

"You're my favorite president!" said Emily, who will fall for anything.

"May I be the speaker at your graduation?" asked Mrs. Roopy, I mean Teddy Roosevelt. "I'll tell you stories of my days as a trust buster."

Trust buster? I didn't know what he was talking about. I looked at Ryan. Ryan looked at Alexia. Alexia looked at Neil. Neil looked at Andrea. We were all looking at each other.

"I'll tell you what," Teddy Roosevelt said. "You kids think it over. I have to go bust some trusts."

Huh? What's a trust? And why would anybody want to bust one?

Teddy Roosevelt ran out of the room. A few minutes later, Mrs. Roopy came back, wearing her regular clothes.

"Okay, I finished my phone call," she told us. "As I was saying, we're going to have a guest speaker at your graduation—"

"Teddy Roosevelt was just here!" Emily shouted excitedly. "He said he had to go bust some trusts."

"Really?" said Mrs. Roopy. "Teddy Roosevelt is my hero! I've got to go get his autograph before he leaves the building."

She went running out of the room again.

A few minutes later, Mrs. Roopy came back. She had gray hair and was wearing a plain black dress and granny glasses.

"Who are you dressed up as *now*, Mrs. Roopy?" asked Andrea.

"Who's Mrs. Roopy?" replied Mrs. Roopy. "My name is Susan B. Anthony. I was one of the first leaders in the fight for women's rights."

"Cool!" said Emily, who believes anything that anybody says.

"May I be the speaker at your graduation?" asked Mrs. Roopy, I mean Susan B. Anthony.

I looked at Michael. Michael looked at Emily. Emily looked at Andrea.

Andrea looked at Ryan. We were all looking at each other.

"You kids think it over," said Susan B. Anthony. "I have to go fight for women's suffrage."

"You want women to suffer?" I asked.

"She said *suffrage*, dumbhead!" Andrea said. "It means the right to vote."

"I knew that," I lied.

Susan B. Anthony ran out of the room. A few minutes later, Mrs. Roopy came back. She was wearing her regular clothes again.

"Ooooh, look!" she said, waving a piece of paper. "I got Teddy Roosevelt's autograph! It was so exciting. I'm sweating."

"Mrs. Roopy!" shouted Emily. "You missed it! Susan B. Anthony was right here in the media center!"

"No way!" said Mrs. Roopy. "She's my hero! This is so upsetting. Oh, dear. I have to go, uh . . . powder my nose."

She went running out of the room again.

"Why would anybody put powder on their nose?" I asked.

"She isn't powdering her nose, dumbhead," said Andrea. "She went to the bathroom. When grown-ups don't want to say they need to go to the bathroom, they say they have to powder their noses."

Grown-ups are weird.

I was going to say something mean to

Andrea, but I didn't get the chance because Mrs. Roopy came running back into the room. This time, she was dressed as an old man with white hair and a bow tie.

"Who are you *now*, Mrs. Roopy?" asked Alexia.

"Who's Mrs. Roopy?" said Mrs. Roopy. "I'm Thomas Edison. I invented the light

bulb, the phonograph, and lots of other things."

"Wow!" said Emily.

"May I be the speaker at your graduation?" asked Mrs. Roopy, I mean Thomas Edison.

"Wait a minute. Isn't

Thomas Edison dead?" asked Ryan.

"*All* those people are dead," said Alexia. "How could *any* of them speak at our graduation?"

"You know what they say," said Thomas Edison, "you can accomplish *anything* if you put your mind to it. That's how I got to be a great inventor. Oh, that reminds me. I have an idea for a new invention. Gotta run!"

Thomas Edison ran out of the room. A minute later, Mrs. Roopy came back.

"Now, as I was saying—"

"Thomas Edison was here!" shouted Emily.

"Really?" asked Mrs. Roopy. "He's my hero!"

"Yes!" said Emily. "He asked us if he could speak at our graduation. So did Susan B. Anthony and Teddy Roosevelt."

"What do you kids think?" asked Mrs. Roopy. "Which one of those people would you like to be the guest speaker?"

"I don't want Teddy Roosevelt," said Ryan.

"I don't want Susan B. Anthony," said Neil.

"I don't want *any* of those old-timey dead people," said Alexia.

"Well, who *do* you kids want to be the speaker at graduation?" asked Mrs. Roopy.

I thought about it for a minute.

"Joseph Gayetty," I said.

Everybody looked at me.

"Who's Joseph Gayetty?" asked Mrs. Roopy.

"He was the guy who invented toilet paper," I explained.*

"I don't think Joseph Gayetty will be

*That's a true fact. Look it up if you don't believe me. I know a lot about toilets.

available to speak at your graduation," said Mrs. Roopy.

Probably not. He's dead too. He invented toilet paper back in 1857. Don't ask me what people used before then.

"Does anybody have another idea for a guest speaker?" asked Mrs. Roopy.

"How about Mother Teresa?" suggested Emily.

"She's dead," said Mrs. Roopy.

"How about Martin Luther King Jr.?" suggested Alexia.

"Also dead," said Mrs. Roopy.

"How about Neil Armstrong?" suggested Neil. "He was the first man on the moon."

"Dead," said Mrs. Roopy.

Bummer in the summer! All the good ones are dead. But that's when I came up with the greatest idea in the history of the world.

"You know who we should get to speak at our graduation?" I said. "Lil Mouse."

"Lil Mouse!" said Ryan. "I love Lil Mouse!"

"Lil Mouse is the coolest," said Michael.

"Yeah, can we get Lil Mouse to speak at graduation?" asked Alexia.

"LIL MOUSE! LIL MOUSE! LIL MOUSE!" we all started chanting.

Chanting is cool.

"Who's Lil Mouse?" asked Mrs. Roopy.

We all laughed. Everybody knows

who Lil Mouse is. Well, every *kid* knows. Lil Mouse is the most popular singer and rapper in the world. Kids love him because he's really cool. Grown-ups love him because he doesn't say bad words. He always wears a mouse costume, so nobody knows what he looks like. His newest rap, "The Happy Little Clam," is all over the internet. We told Mrs. Roopy all about Lil Mouse.

"I'm sorry," she said, "but Mrs. Stoker would never let me have a rapper be the speaker at your graduation. Besides, it would cost a fortune to get a famous person like that. We don't have money to pay for a speaker. And Lil Mouse is probably too busy anyway."

"BOOOOOOOOOOOOOOOO!"

Everybody started booing. No fair! Kids never get to decide *anything*. It's *our* graduation. *We* should be allowed to pick the guest speaker. Bummer in the summer!

This was going to be the worst graduation in the history of graduations.

A Face in
the Woods

While we were eating lunch in the vomi-torium that day, everybody was bummed about graduation. Nobody had much to say. During recess, we all just sat around the monkey bars in the playground. I didn't even want to go to graduation. It was sure to be a big snoozefest.

That's when the weirdest thing in the history of the world happened.

But I'm not going to tell you what it was.

Okay, okay, I'll tell you.

I was hanging upside down on the monkey bars when I noticed something in the woods behind the playground. Just as the wind blew against the trees, I caught a glimpse of something—or someone.

"What was that?" I said, pointing to the woods.

"What was *what*?" asked Ryan.

"I just saw a face in the trees over there," I said as I hopped down off the monkey bars. I peered into the woods, but I couldn't see the face anymore.

"What did he look like?" asked Michael.

"I don't know if it was a *he*," I replied. "I think the person was wearing a hat and looking through binoculars."

"Maybe it's a robber," said Neil.

"Maybe it's an international supervillain who wants to take over the world," said Michael, who thinks everybody wants to take over the world.

"Stop trying to scare Emily," said Andrea.

"I'm scared," whimpered Emily.

"Maybe it's Amelia Earhart," suggested Ryan.

Amelia Earhart was a lady who was trying to fly a plane around the world. She disappeared and nobody knows what happened to her.

"I think the blood was rushing to your head, A.J.," said Alexia. "Maybe it was just a mirage."

"Yes, you were probably just seeing things, Arlo," said Andrea.

"I wasn't seeing things!" I insisted. "I was seeing somebody hiding in the woods!"

"We should tell Officer Spence, the secu-rity guard," said Ryan.

"Ryan," I said. "Let's go look for ourselves. Come on, follow me."

Everybody climbed down off the monkey bars and followed me across the soccer field. I figured we should sneak over to the side and come around the back so the mysterious person in the woods wouldn't see us coming.

You are one-of-a-kind! And you are loved!

33

We were slinking around on our tiptoes, like secret agents. It was cool.

"Okay, everybody be quiet," I whispered as we made our way through the woods.

"What if it's a monster?" asked Neil.

"I'm scared," whined Emily.

"Shhhhhhh!" I shushed.

We slinked through the trees, being careful not to step on anything that would make noise. I didn't see anybody hiding out there.

But then we came to a clearing in the trees.

I saw the back of a person sitting on a rock. It looked like a man. He was peering through binoculars at the playground.

One of us must have made a noise because suddenly the man turned around. And you'll never believe in a million hundred years who was hiding in the woods.

I'm not going to tell you.

Okay, okay, I'll tell you.

It was Mr. Klutz, our old principal!

Betcha didn't see *that* coming!

"Mr. Klutz!" we all shouted.

A few months ago, Mr. Klutz was forced to retire by Dr. Carbles, the president of the Board of Education. He's a mean man who drives a tank to school. Dr. Carbles hired Mrs. Stoker to be the new principal.

I almost didn't recognize Mr. Klutz because he had grown a beard. That was

weird, because it means he can grow hair on the bottom of his head but not on the top. What's up with that? Instead of growing a beard, it would have been cool if he just turned his head upside down.

We all gathered around to give Mr. Klutz a hug.

"We missed you!" we all said.

"I missed you too!" said Mr. Klutz.

"What are you doing out here in the woods?" asked Michael. "And what's with the binoculars?"

"Oh, this?" said Mr. Klutz. "Uh . . . I'm . . . uh . . . bird-watching. Yes, that's it! Uh, bird-watching! It's my new hobby since I retired. I, uh . . . just spotted a red-billed oxpecker."

Obviously, Mr. Klutz was lying. You can always tell somebody is lying when they say "uh" too much.

"Why don't you come to the playground and say hello?" asked Andrea. "Everybody will be happy to see you again."

"Yeah!" we all agreed.

"I can't," Mr. Klutz whispered to us. "I'm not allowed on school grounds. Dr. Carbles got a restraining order against me."

"Not fair!" said Ryan.

"Are you enjoying your retirement?" asked Andrea.

"Oh, I, uh . . . love it," Mr. Klutz replied. "It's, uh . . . the greatest. I love being retired. It's so much fun. I couldn't be, uh . . . happier."

38

And then, suddenly, he burst into tears.

Clearly, Mr. Klutz didn't love being retired.

It was sad to watch him cry. Soon, Emily was crying too. Then Neil started crying. Then Ryan and Michael started crying. Then Alexia and Andrea started crying.

Then I started crying. We were *all* crying.

"You're too young to retire," said Alexia.

"I miss Ella Mentry School so much," Mr. Klutz blubbered. "Please don't tell anyone I was crying. Don't tell anyone you saw me out here."

"Your secret is safe with us," I said.

We group-hugged again. And at that moment . . .

Brrriiiiinnnnnngggg!

Yes, the school bell sounds like *Brrriiiiinnnnnngggg!* Nobody knows why.

Recess was over.*

---

*Hey, when is Lil Mouse gonna show up? His name is on the cover of the book.

Mrs. Stoker Is a Joker

When we got back to our classroom, Mr. Cooper wasn't there yet, so of course I climbed up on my chair and shook my butt at everybody.

"Arlo, sit down," said Andrea, rolling her eyes.

"Chillax," I told Little Miss Perfect. "It's

June. School will be over in a few days. We're allowed to goof off."

And you'll never believe who walked into the door at that moment.

Nobody! Why would you walk into a door? You could break your nose. But you'll never believe who walked into the door*way*.

It was our new principal, Mrs. Stoker!

I thought she was going to punish me for climbing up on my chair and shaking my butt at the class. But she didn't.

"Hey, third grade!" Mrs. Stoker said cheerfully. "Are you excited about graduation?"

"Yes!" shouted all the girls.

"No!" shouted all the boys.

"That reminds me," said Mrs. Stoker, "do you know why M&Ms want to graduate?"

"No, why?" we all said.

"So they can turn into Smarties!" said Mrs. Stoker. "Get it?"

We all laughed even though it wasn't funny. You should always laugh at the principal's jokes, even when they're not funny. That's the first rule of being a kid.

"Speaking of graduation," said Mrs. Stoker, "I may have to wear sunglasses to the ceremony. Because you're all so bright! Get it? Bright? Sunglasses?"

"We get it," we all said.

Before she was our principal, Mrs. Stoker was a stand-up comedian. She tells jokes all the time.

"Do you know why the fish didn't graduate?" asked Mrs. Stoker.

"Because it didn't show up for school?"
I guessed.*

"No," said Mrs. Stoker. "The fish didn't graduate because its grades were under C. Get it? Under C? Undersea?"

After a few more of Mrs. Stoker's bad jokes, it became harder and harder to pretend they were funny.

"Tall people graduate at the top of their class," continued Mrs. Stoker, "and Mr. Will, the ice-cream man, graduated from sundae school. Get it? Ice cream? Sundae school?"

I thought she was *never* going to stop.

---

*I thought that was pretty genius because fish swim around in schools.

But finally she did.

"Anyway," said Mrs. Stoker, "I heard you kids were planning your graduation. I just thought I'd stop in to see how you were making out."

Ewwww! Gross!

"We're not planning our graduation," said Alexia. "Mrs. Roopy is doing all the work. She wants us to have Teddy Roosevelt, Susan B. Anthony, or Thomas Edison be our guest speaker."

"What's wrong with them?" asked Mrs. Stoker. "They are great American heroes."

"We don't want some boring old dead person," I said.

"Yeah, it's not fair!" agreed Ryan.

"Well, who do *you* want to speak at your graduation?" asked Mrs. Stoker.

"We want Lil Mouse," said Neil.

I figured Mrs. Stoker wouldn't know who Lil Mouse was because she's old, and old people don't know anything.

"Do you mean Lil Mouse, the rapper?" asked Mrs. Stoker.

"You've heard of Lil Mouse?" I asked.

"Sure!" said Mrs. Stoker. "You may not believe this, but Lil Mouse is my nephew."

WHAT?!

"No way!" said Michael.

"Yes way!" replied Mrs. Stoker.

"Wait," said Alexia. "Is this another one of your jokes?"

"No!" Mrs. Stoker said as she took out her smartphone and showed us a picture of Lil Mouse. "He's my brother's son."

"I love Lil Mouse!" said Andrea.

"Me too!" said Emily, who loves anything Andrea loves.

"*Everybody* loves Lil Mouse," said Neil.

"Would you like me to invite Lil Mouse to speak at graduation?" asked Mrs. Stoker.

"Yes!" shouted all the girls.

"Yes!" shouted all the boys.

Mrs. Stoker took out her smartphone again and typed a few words on the keypad.

"You have Lil Mouse's cell phone number?" asked Alexia.

"Of course!" Mrs. Stoker replied. "I'm his favorite aunt. He's in the middle of a world tour. He may not be able to make it to graduation. But it can't hurt to ask, right?"

"Cool!" we all shouted.

When she finished typing her text, she

pushed SEND and told us that Lil Mouse usually replied back to her in a day or two. But a few seconds later, her phone beeped.

"Excuse me," she said. "Somebody is texting me. Oh, it's from Lil Mouse!"

"What did he say?" we all hollered.

"He says . . . he'll *do* it!" said Mrs. Stoker.

"YAY!" we all shouted.

Everybody was yelling and screaming and hooting and hollering and jumping up and down. Lil Mouse was going to be the guest speaker! It was the greatest day of my life. We were going to have the best graduation in the history of graduations.

The Happy Little Clam

When I was a little kid—about a year ago—my favorite singer was this teenage rapper named Cray-Z. You may have heard of him. He had this really famous song about a guy named Klepto from the South Pole who comes down your chimney on Christmas Eve and steals everybody's presents.* It ends like this . . .

*The name's Klepto and I'm from the
South Pole. I grab all your presents.
That's how I roll.*

*On Christmas Eve, I go 'round the
world, and steal all the presents
from boys and girls.*

"The Christmas Klepto" was probably
the biggest hit in the history of music.
Everybody was singing it during the holi-
days. Cray-Z was on a bunch of TV shows.
Girls would scream their heads off as soon

---

*You can read about it in a book called *Deck the Halls,
We're Off the Walls!*

as they saw him. Cray-Z was so famous, even grown-ups knew all about him.

Well, that was last year. Nobody listens to Cray-Z anymore. I heard that he dropped out of school and was working at a car wash.

Now, the hottest singer in the world is Lil Mouse. He's all over the internet and he is *so* cool. All his songs are about animals, and he dances around dressed as a mouse while he's singing. He's got songs about giraffes, sea turtles, and orangutans. Lil Mouse is more famous than Cray-Z ever was. That's why he wears a mouse costume. If people knew what he really looked like, Lil Mouse wouldn't be able to step outside without being mobbed by fans.

Lil Mouse's newest song is "The Happy Little Clam." It goes like this . . .

I'm happy as a clam.
I'm happy as a clam.
Who decided clams are happy?
I say it's a sham.

What's the deal with clams?
I don't understand.
They live in dirty water
and they don't have hands.

I'm happy as I am.
Don't wanna be a clam.
I'd rather be a lamb,
or a ham,
or a ram,
or a yam,
or just about anything but a clam.

Lemme give you a clue.
Here's some things clams can't do.
They can't play ball
or go to the mall.

They can't sing a song

or play Ping-Pong.

They can't make pottery.

Can't win the lottery.

They can't build a dam.

They can't ride a tram,

or hit a grand slam,

or pass an exam.

They can't even post on Instagram.

Go for a walk?

Fly like a hawk?

They can't even talk!

Maybe I'm spoiled

'cause I've never been boiled.

In my dreams, I don't get steamed,

baked, broiled, pickled, or fried.

If I was a clam, I'd go and hide.

No, thank you, ma'am.

Don't wanna be a clam.

Can't say it any louder.

Don't wanna be a chowder.

I don't know why

we say they're happy.

Seems to me

clam lives are @#$%^&!

Cool song, huh? I heard that Lil Mouse made up "The Happy Little Clam" in his bedroom one morning. Then he recorded it before lunch that day and posted it on the internet. The song went viral, and by dinnertime Lil Mouse was just about the most famous person in the history of the world.

When I grow up, I want to be a rapper like Lil Mouse. And he's going to be speaking at our graduation!

Man, life is good.

Fourth Grade Is Scary

"Okay, everybody," said Mr. Cooper, "take out a pencil."

Ugh. That meant it was time for writing. I hate writing.*

"I'm passing out . . ." said Mr. Cooper.

"He's passing out!" I shouted. "Call an ambulance!"

---

*I don't even know why I'm writing this.

" . . . pieces of paper. So each of you can write an essay."

Ugh! Writing essays is mega-boring. Mr. Cooper told us to write about what we were planning to do over summer vacation.

"I'm going to sleepaway camp!" Andrea said excitedly.

"Me too!" said Emily, who does everything Andrea does.

Ryan said his family would be going to the beach. Michael said his cousins were coming to visit. Alexia said she would be going to Puerto Rico. Everybody started writing.

I didn't know what to write. How should I know what I'm going to do over summer vacation? It wasn't even summer yet. I sat

there for a million hundred minutes trying to think of something to write.

"Five more minutes," said Mr. Cooper.

Those five minutes felt like an hour.
Andrea filled *two* sheets of paper, of
course. Finally, Mr. Cooper picked up our
papers.

"What's wrong, A.J.?" he asked as he
looked at mine. "There's nothing on your
paper."

"That's because I'm planning to do
nothing over the summer," I told him. "So
that's what I wrote. Nothing."

Everybody laughed even though I
didn't say anything funny. That's when an
announcement came over the loudspeaker.

"Mr. Cooper, please call the front office."

Mr. Cooper picked up the phone. While he was on his call, the rest of us whispered to each other.

"I hear we're going to get lockers in fourth grade," whispered Alexia. "So we'll have to memorize our locker combination."

"I hear," whispered Neil, "that if you forget your locker combination the teacher locks you up in your locker all night."

"Stop trying to scare Emily," whispered Andrea.

"I'm scared," whispered Emily.

"I hear," whispered Ryan, "that in fourth grade we're going to get five hours of homework each night."

"I hear," whispered Michael, "they make fourth graders do math with letters instead of numbers."

"What?" I whispered. "That's crazy. You can't add up letters."

"It's called algebra," whispered Andrea. "I'm taking an algebra class after school."

Andrea takes classes in *everything* after school. If they gave classes in how to tie your shoes, Andrea would take that class so she could get better at it.

"I hear," whispered Neil, "in fourth grade we have to bring toothpaste to school with us."

"I hear," whispered Alexia, "the fifth graders are going to shoot spitballs at us."

"I hear," I whispered, "that they're going to shoot bowling balls at us. With cata-pults."

Actually, I've never heard that fifth

graders shoot bowling balls at fourth graders with catapults. I just made that up to scare Emily.

"I'm scared," whispered Emily.

Mr. Cooper hung up the phone.

"I have an announcement to make," he said. "The front office just told me the name of the third-grade valedictorian."

Valedic . . . *WHAT*?

"What's that?" I asked. "It sounds like some disease."

"The valedictorian," said Mr. Cooper, "is the student who achieves the highest rank in the class. Our class valedictorian will be . . . Andrea!"

Everybody clapped as the Human Homework Machine smiled the smile she smiles to let everyone know she knows something that nobody else knows. I bet Miss Smarty Pants has been waiting for this moment her whole life.

In the days leading up to graduation, I had to do all kinds of boring stuff. I had to go clothes shopping to get a jacket and tie (ugh) so I'd look good for my graduation picture (ugh).

I had to get a cap and gown too. Why do graduates have to wear a dorky cap with a big square on top of it? What's up with that? Why does putting a square on your head mean you're smart? I say they should make the dumbest kids wear squares on their heads, and when they graduate they get to take the squares *off.* That would make more sense.

It was a horrible week. We had to spend every day practicing for graduation by lining up in ABC order. Ugh. It would have been more interesting to watch a turtle race. I couldn't wait for graduation . . . so we could get it over with.

Blah Blah Blah . . .

It was graduation day. At last! I didn't care much about graduation, but I couldn't wait to see Lil Mouse live and in person.

After I woke up, I brushed my teeth and put on my cap and gown. Then I went downstairs for breakfast.

"I look ridorkulous," I announced to my parents.

"You're right, for once," said my big sister, Amy.

"Don't be silly," said my dad. "You look very handsome, A.J."

"We are so proud of you, A.J.," said my mother. She looked like she was going to start crying.

"It's just third grade, Mom!" I told her. "It's not like I'm graduating from college."

"Ha!" snorted Amy. "As if *that's* ever gonna happen."

We drove to school and went in the side entrance to the all-porpoise room. I don't know why they call it the all-porpoise room. There are no dolphins in there. But the room was filled with teachers and parents and grandparents and great-grandparents and aunts and uncles and brothers and sisters and a bunch of other people who looked like they just showed up because they had nothing better to do.

Some of the moms from the PTA* were selling hot cross buns. The rest of the parents were taking pictures. Of course. Parents *love* taking pictures.

"Oh no," I groaned. "Not pictures!"

"This is a milestone, A.J.," my dad said.

Everything is a milestone with parents. I could clip my toenails and my parents would say it was a milestone. Then they'd take pictures of me clipping my toenails.

---

*Parents who Talk Alot.

Ryan's and Michael's parents were taking pictures next to us, so of course the grown-ups had to gather the three of us together for a group shot.

"Don't they look handsome?" said Michael's mom.

"Smile!" all the parents shouted.

First they took pictures of me and Ryan and Michael. Then they took pictures of me and Michael. Then they took pictures of me and Ryan. Then they took pictures of Ryan and Michael. Then they took selfies of themselves with me and Ryan and Michael in the background.

Ugh. I thought I was gonna die from old age.

"Hey, let's get the brothers and sisters in there!" shouted my dad.

"No!" shouted me and Ryan and Michael.

My dad once told me that when he was a kid in prehistoric times, people couldn't take a million hundred pictures of every little thing they did. Cameras needed this stuff called film, and when you ran out of film, you couldn't take any more pictures. I miss the good old days, before I was born.

Finally, the picture-taking torture was over. The parents were sobbing and blowing their noses into tissues. Well, they were blowing their *snot* into the tissues. It could be dangerous to blow your whole nose into a tissue.

"I can't believe my baby Ryan is graduating from third grade," blubbered Ryan's mom. "It seems like only yesterday he was in diapers."

"Dude," I said to Ryan, "you wore diapers yesterday?"

We were told to take our seats up on the stage. I had to sit between annoying Andrea and crybaby Emily. Alexia and Neil were sitting in the row behind me.

"Where's Lil Mouse?" Neil asked me.

I looked around. Lil Mouse was *not* in the house.

"Celebrities always show up late," I told Neil. "That way they can make a grand entrance."

Principal Stoker stepped up to the mic and made a peace sign with her fingers, which means "shut up." Everybody got quiet.

"Welcome, third graders!" said Mrs. Stoker. "I have a question for you. What's brown, hairy, and wears sunglasses?"

"What?" we all shouted.

"A coconut on vacation!" said Mrs. Stoker, and then she doubled over laughing. "But seriously, kids, what kind of tree fits in your hand?"

"I give up," we all shouted.

"A palm tree!" said Mrs. Stoker. "Get it? Okay enough jokes. Before we give out your diplomas, some of your teachers would like to say a few words."

One by one, teachers went up to the mic and said how proud they were of us.

"*Blah blah blah . . .*" said Ms. Hannah, our art teacher.

"*Blah blah blah . . .*" said Mr. Docker, our science teacher.

"*Blah blah blah . . .*" said Mrs. Yonkers, our computer teacher.

"*Blah blah blah . . .*" said Miss Small, our fizz ed teacher.

"*Blah blah blah . . .*" said Mr. Macky, our reading specialist.

They went on and on. Even Mr. Burke, the guy who mows the lawn, got up to say a few words.

Ugh. I was bored already. It would have been more interesting to watch glaciers race. And still, there was no sign of Lil Mouse.

"I don't think Lil Mouse is gonna show," Alexia whispered to me.

"He'll be here," I assured her. "He's probably in his limo right now. Or maybe he's coming by helicopter."

Famous people take helicopters all the time. Nobody knows why.

"And now," announced Mrs. Stoker, "I would like to introduce your third-grade valedictorian . . . Andrea Young!"

Ugh. Smarty pants Andrea got up and went over to the mic. Little Miss Perfect was smiling the smile she smiles to let everybody know she knows something nobody else knows. She took a sheet of paper out of her pocket.

"Thank you, Mrs. Stoker," said Miss Know-It-All as she looked around at the audience. "Parents . . . teachers . . . fellow students. I am truly honored to be your valedictorian *blah blah blah* . . ."

Andrea went on and on.

"This doesn't mean I'm smarter than you. This doesn't mean I'm better than you. This doesn't mean that I have a brighter future ahead of me than you do. Well, maybe it does. It's hard to tell *blah blah blah . . ."*

She went on and on . . .

"I worked really hard this year. While you were goofing off and playing video games, I was studying. While you were wasting time watching YouTube, I was

taking classes after school and reading *The Complete Works of Shakespeare*. I worked hard while everyone else was making fun of me for being smart. Well, who's laughing now? I'll be thinking of you when I'm at Harvard someday. My fellow classmates, I have one piece of advice. Keep your nose to the grindstone."

Huh? What's a grindstone? Why would I want to put my face on a rock? And why can't a truck full of grindstones fall on Andrea's head?

"I want to finish," Andrea continued, "by thanking all the people that made this possible. My teachers—Miss Daisy, Mr. Granite, and Mr. Cooper. My parents.

All the tutors at my after-school pro-grams. I want to thank Noah Webster for writing the dictionary, which I read every day. But most of all, I want to thank myself. Because if it hadn't been for me, I wouldn't be standing here today. Thank me. I mean you."

Everybody clapped while Andrea went back to her seat, smiling her annoying smile.

The graduation torture was almost fin-ished. Mrs. Stoker went over to the mic again.

"And now, third graders, this is the moment you've all been waiting for . . ."

Lil Mouse finally arrived?

" . . . it's time to hand out the diplomas," said Mrs. Stoker.

Oh, yeah. I forgot about diplomas.

But that's when the weirdest thing in the history of the world happened. Suddenly, the lights in the all-porpoise room dimmed. There was the sound of an explosion. Music started playing. Colored laser beams flashed all over the place. The door to the back of the all-porpoise room swung open.

I heard somebody shout . . .

Lil Mouse Is in the House!

Everybody went crazy when Lil Mouse came running into the all-porpoise room.

"Yo! Yo! Yo!" he shouted.

Rappers always say "Yo!" Nobody knows why.

"And now . . ." said Mrs. Stoker, "it's time . . . for our guest speaker . . . put your hands together . . . for my nephew . . . Lil Mouse!"

There was a roar like a jet engine in the all-porpoise room.

"DO THE MOUSE!" kids started chanting. "DO THE MOUSE!"

Lil Mouse ran to the front of the room and jumped on the stage. He did the Mouse dance for a few seconds, and then he grabbed the mic and started rapping . . .

I'm happy as a clam.
I'm happy as a clam.
Who decided clams are happy?
I say it's a sham.

Life ain't so grand
when you're living in the sand.
Life is a dud
when you live in mud and crud . . .

"Hey, that's not how 'The Happy Little Clam' goes," Neil yelled in my ear.

Don't wanna be a clam,
Sam I am.
It's not my jam.
I'd rather read my spam
than be a clam.

"He must have forgotten the words," I shouted to Neil.

"I thought Lil Mouse was a lot shorter," Neil replied.

If I was a clam, I'd sit and pout.
What are clams so happy about?
They can't go to Amsterdam
or Birmingham.
They can't even go to Disneyland
unless they're fried.

"That doesn't even rhyme," Andrea said.

"You know what?" I said. "I don't think that's Lil Mouse!"

"He's a phony!" somebody shouted.

A happy clam?
I say that's a sham.
It's a flim-flam scam.
The flim-flam clam scam.

"That's a fake Lil Mouse!" shouted Michael.

"This guy is terrible," said Ryan.

"Fake! Fake! Fake!" kids started chanting.

Oh, please. Oh, please.
Clams live in filthy seas.

They don't have legs
and of course they don't have knees.

"We want the *real* Lil Mouse!" shouted
Alexia.

"Yeah!" somebody else shouted.

"BOOOOOOOOOOOO!"

Everybody started booing.

From what I hear,

clams are really selfish.

Well, what do you expect

from a bunch of shellfish?

You never see 'em peeing.

They can't go skiing.

They can't join the air force.

They're just a food source . . .

"BOOOOOOOOOOOO!"

"Get him off the stage!"

"I bet it's Mrs. Roopy," I said. "She's always pretending to be other people."

I looked around. All of our teachers were there, but not Mrs. Roopy. It had to be her. She must be dressed up as Lil Mouse.

"It's Mrs. Roopy in disguise!" I yelled.

"BOOOOOOOOOOOOO!"

We were drowning out Lil Mouse. He stopped rapping.

And you'll never believe in a million hundred years who walked into the door at that moment.

Nobody! It would hurt if you walked into a door. But you'll never believe who walked into the door*way*.

It was Mrs. Roopy!

WHAT?!

"Sorry I'm late," announced Mrs. Roopy. "I was stuck in traffic."

"Wait a minute," I said. "If Mrs. Roopy is here and Lil Mouse is also here, that means Mrs. Roopy cannot be Lil Mouse!"

"Gee, Arlo," said Andrea, "you're a real genius. No wonder you're in the gifted and talented program."

I was going to say something mean to Andrea, but I didn't get the chance because Mrs. Stoker ran over to Lil Mouse. She reached up and pulled off his ridorkulous mouse head.

And you'll never believe in a million hundred years who was dressed up as Lil Mouse.

It was Mr. Klutz, our old principal!

WHAT?!

"I *knew* it was a fake!" shouted Michael.

"Mr. Klutz!" shouted Mrs. Roopy. "What

are *you* doing here?"

"I had to be here," Mr. Klutz replied. "I love these kids. I couldn't miss their graduation. This was the only way I could sneak into the building."

That's when the weirdest thing in the history of the world happened. You'll never believe who walked into the door at that moment.

Nobody! Didn't we go over this already?

But you'll never believe who walked into the door*way*.

It was Dr. Carbles, the president of the Board of Education!

WHAT?!

Dr. Carbles looked around and saw Mr. Klutz.

"Klutz!" he shouted. "I told you to stay off school grounds! What are you doing in that mouse costume?"

"But . . . but . . . but . . ."

We all giggled because Mr. Klutz said "but," which sounds just like "butt" even though it only has one *T*.

"Gotta run!" said Mr. Klutz, and he ran off the stage.

Dr. Carbles chased him out of the all-porpoise room. He was screaming all the way down the hallway.

"I'll get you, Klutz! This is the last straw!"

Huh? What did straws have to do with anything?

* * *

After all that excitement, it was quiet in the all-porpoise room. I had a moment to think about what had happened. And that's when it hit me. Mrs. Stoker must have been lying to us the whole time! She wasn't Lil Mouse's aunt. She probably didn't even *know* Lil Mouse.

"You lied to us!" I shouted at her. "Lil Mouse isn't really your nephew!"

"He is too!" she shouted back. "You've got to believe me! Lil Mouse told me he would come to your graduation, but his flight home from England was canceled. So I asked Mr. Klutz to take his place. I'm so sorry."

Then Mrs. Stoker started crying.

"Liar! Liar! Liar!" everybody started chanting.

That's when the weirdest thing in the history of the world happened. You'll never believe who walked into the door at that moment.*

It was Lil Mouse! The *real* Lil Mouse!

"LIL MOUSE IS IN THE HOUSE!" he shouted.

He ran over and gave Mrs. Stoker a hug.

"I felt so bad after my flight was canceled," he told her. "I rented a private jet so I could be here! I couldn't let down my favorite aunt! Is it too late for me to sing a song?"

"NO!" everybody shouted.

---

*Do we really have to go through this again?

"DO THE MOUSE!" we all chanted. "DO THE MOUSE!"

Lil Mouse did The Mouse. Then he grabbed the microphone and started rapping . . .

I'm happy as a clam.
I'm happy as a clam.
Who decided clams are happy?
I say it's a sham . . .

Well, you know the rest of the song.

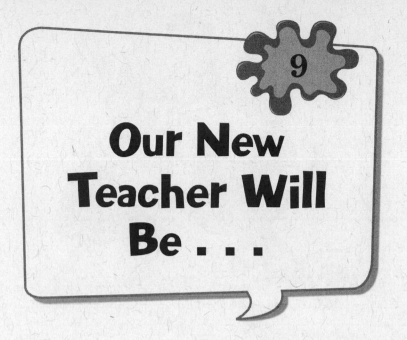

Our New Teacher Will Be . . .

I have some good news and some bad news.

The good news is that thanks to Lil Mouse, we had the greatest graduation in the history of graduations. It was the end of an era at Ella Mentry School. We were officially fourth graders.

And now for the bad news. The day after graduation, some new rapper named Big Mouse recorded a song in his bathroom, and an hour later it went viral. Suddenly, Lil Mouse was old news, and his career was over. Mrs. Stoker told us he's working at a car wash with Cray-Z.

Hey, who said stories have to have a

happy ending? Deal with it.

Maybe Lil Mouse will write another hit song. Maybe we'll get a new math book in fourth grade. Maybe Teddy Roosevelt will bust some trusts, whatever they are. Maybe grown-ups will stop powdering their noses. Maybe I'll find out what people used before toilet paper was invented. Maybe Mr. Klutz will turn his head upside down. Maybe Ryan will stop wearing diapers. Maybe we'll find out why they changed the name of the library. Maybe people will stop walking into doors all the time. Maybe somebody will figure out why clams are so happy.

But it won't be easy!

* * *

Oh, I forgot to tell you. After we got our diplomas, Mr. Cooper gathered us all around him in the back of the all-porpoise room.

"Well, this is it," he told us. "It has been my honor to be your third-grade teacher. I'm going to miss you kids."

It looked like Mr. Cooper was going to start crying.*

"We'll miss you too," said Alexia.

We group-hugged for a long time.

"Who will be our teacher in fourth grade?" asked Andrea, who obviously wanted to know who she needed to suck up to.

"I think the list of classroom teachers

---

*Boy, there sure was a lot of crying in this book!

was just posted outside the front office," said Mr. Cooper.

We all rushed to the front office. Mr. Cooper was right. There were a bunch of papers taped to the wall with the names of each teacher and all the kids in each class.

We crowded around to see who our

new teacher would be for fourth grade. There were a million hundred names on the wall. I searched all over to find the name of our new teacher. But Andrea, of course, found it first.

"I'm so excited!" Andrea finally shouted. "It says our new teacher is going to be

TO HARDCORE MY WEIRD SCHOOL FANS

There is a mistake in Chapter 1 of this book. We put it in on

purpose. Did you spot it? The answer will be revealed in the

first book of the next series, My Weirdtastic School.

More weird books from Dan Gutman

My Weird School

My Weird School Graphic Novels

My Weirder School

My Weirdest School
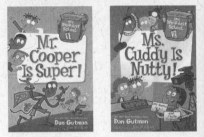

My Weirder-est School

My Weird School Fast Facts

My Weird School Daze

My Weird Tips